Where Do Giggles Come From?

By Diane Muldrow

Illustrated by Anne Kennedy

A GOLDEN BOOK · NEW YORK

Published in the United States by Golden Books, an imprint of Random House Children's Books,
a division of Random House, Inc., 1745 Broadway, New York, NY 10019.
Golden Books, A Golden Book, A Little Golden Book, the G colophon, and the distinctive gold spine
are registered trademarks of Random House, Inc.
www.randomhouse.com/kids
Educators and librarians, for a variety of teaching tools, visit us at www.randomhouse.com/kids
Library of Congress Control Number: 2009933524
ISBN: 978-0-375-86133-8
Printed in the United States of America
20 19 10 17 16 15

I like it when you hula dance.
I love it when you wiggle.
But what I love the most of all . . .

Is your silly, jolly giggle!

You giggle in your bouncy seat

And when you're upside down . . .

When making faces in the mirror
And twirling round and round!

You giggle when we play "piggie toes,"

As well as hide-and-seek.

You giggle when I count to ten
And promise not to peek!

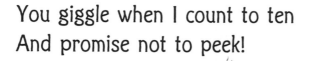

You giggle when you splish and splash

And when you get away.

Oh, I love to get your giggle going
Every single day.

Snuggly kisses make you giggle,

And funny faces, too.

So do chasing butterflies

And playing peek-a-boo.

When you giggle in the sprinkler,
Your tummy shakes like jelly!

But where's that giggle coming from?

From deep inside your belly!